Grigio's Great

Adventures Around the World

Story and Illustrations by:
James O'Brien

I'm dedicating this book to my wife, partner, and best friend. Jill, your support and positivity makes it all possible.

First paperback edition Sept 2024
Book design by James D O'Brien
Edited by Jill O'Brien

ISBN 979-8-218-51720-5 (paperback)

Meet Grigio, the happiest Bernese Mountain Dog in all the land! She loves to dig holes in her backyard—big ones, deep ones, even long tunnels. But Grigio's digging wasn't like any other dog's. Her holes led to magical places all around the world!

One sunny afternoon, Grigio dug deeper than ever before. Suddenly—whoosh!—she fell through the ground and popped out in a land far, far away.

Grigio landed in a colorful place filled with people wearing beautiful, flowing robes. She had arrived in India! The air smelled of spices, and everyone was preparing for a big festival.

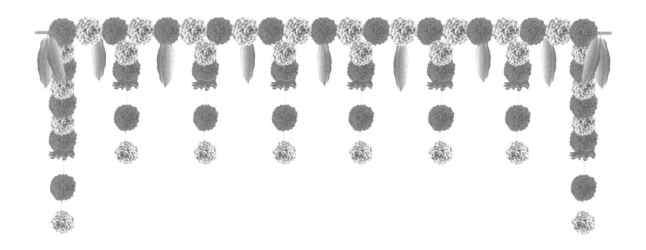

A group of children ran up to Grigio and gave her a flower garland. They were celebrating Holi, the Festival of Colors! Grigio wagged her tail and joined in the fun.

But Grigio wasn't done exploring! She dug another hole and—poof!—she fell through again, this time landing in Mexico.

Grigio found herself on a lively street filled with music and dancing. She had arrived just in time for Día de los Muertos, the Day of the Dead celebration!

Children wearing colorful costumes showed Grigio their beautiful altars, decorated with candles and photos. Grigio sniffed the flowers and happily wagged her tail.

Grigio's next hole took her to Ireland! She landed in the middle of a beautiful green field, with rolling hills and ancient stone walls.

Grigio joined a group of children dancing to lively Irish music. They wore traditional Irish clothing and twirled around in a joyful celebration. Grigio couldn't resist joining in with a wag of her tail!

After chasing the sheep, Grigio was ready for more adventures! She dug a hole and—zoom!— she fell right into Japan

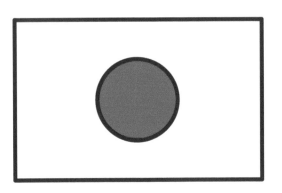

Grigio was surrounded by cherry blossom trees, families on blankets eating sushi, and children playing with kites.

It was time for another trip. Grigio dug another hole and popped out in the warm and sunny country of Brazil.

In Brazil, Grigio joined a carnival parade! People wore bright costumes with feathers and sparkles, and music filled the air. She enjoyed meeting her new friends, Faustina and Sparky.

Feeling adventurous, Grigio dug once more. This time, she found herself in Switzerland, her homeland! She was surrounded by snowy mountains and cozy chalets.

Grigio joined a group of yodelers singing in the snowy town. She even wore a little Swiss hat! Afterward, she pulled her favorite milk wagon and ran through the snow, happily barking and enjoying the crisp air.

After so many adventures, Grigio decided it was time to go home. She dug one last hole and landed back in her cozy backyard. The sun was setting, and everything was calm.

Grigio stretched and yawned,
feeling tired but happy.

Grigio curled up in her bed as the stars twinkled in the night sky. It had been a day full of adventures. Grigio drifted off to sleep, and dreamed of all the places she had been. Her paws twitched as she imagined digging more holes, leading to new adventures in the world.

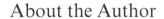

About the Author

James D. O'Brien "Shamus" hails from Farmington, Connecticut, and is an artist, using his life experiences and artwork to inspire his storytelling. This children's book marks his first venture into writing, developed from a simple moment with Grigio, his dog, digging in the yard. As a child, James often imagined digging holes that led to faraway places—a fantasy that has now come to life in his book.

When James isn't busy painting with oil or gouache, he enjoys spending time with his wife Jill, grandchildren, taking short frustrating walks with his dogs, or hitting the golf course. This book is a heartfelt way for James to share his creativity and leave a lasting legacy for his family.

To connect with James, follow him on Instagram @jamesd.obrien

Printed in the USA
CPSIA information can be obtained
at www.ICGtesting.com
LVHW071759221024
794530LV00002B/3